SMALLER SISTER

MAGGIE EDKINS WILLIS

Roaring Brook Press
New York

For Katie

Published by Roaring Brook Press. Roaring Brook Press is a division of Holtzbrinck Publishing Holdings Limited Partnership.
120 Broadway, New York, NY 10271 · mackids.com
Text and illustrations copyright © 2022 by Maggie Edkins Willis.
All rights reserved.
Our books may be purchased in bulk for promotional, educational, or business use. Please contact your local bookseller or the Macmillan Corporate and Premium Sales Department at (800) 221-7945 ext. 5442 or by email at MacmillanSpecialMarkets@macmillan.com.
Library of Congress Cataloging-in-Publication Data is available.
First edition, 2022. Cover design by Kirk Benshoff.
Interior book design by Molly Johanson and Maggie Edkins Willis.
The illustrations for this book were painted digitally.
Printed in China by Toppan Leefung Printing Ltd.,
Dongguan City, Guangdong Province.
ISBN 978-1-250-76741-7 (hardcover)
1 3 5 7 9 10 8 6 4 2
ISBN 978-1-250-76742-4 (paperback)
1 3 5 7 9 10 8 6 4 2

Content warning:
This book contains eating disorder thoughts and behaviors

CHAPTER 1

Of course, our relationship wasn't perfect.

CRACK

SECRET SISTER CODE TRANSLATION:

Dear Lucy, I'm sorry I broke the crayon. Can we play mermaids instead? Love, Olivia

9

Are mermaids fish or are they people?

PLEASE go to sleep.

Okay.

I wish I had a sleeping potion.

AARRGH!!!

Olivia **REALLY** wanted her own room.

SADIE CORINA BAILEY

At school, Olivia was shy, but she'd had the same tight group of girlfriends since kindergarten. They played on the same basketball team and had sleepovers every weekend. They were a year older than me in age, but sometimes it felt like they were a thousand years older than me in coolness.

Sure you don't want a slice, Livy?

Nah, I'm good.

Her friends were always nice to me, but Olivia hated it when I tagged along. So I taught myself to be invisible.

Bailey, I think DeVon has a crush on you.

No way! He's just my neighbor's grandson so he hangs out at our house a lot.

Yeah, but he *also* likes you.

Liv, do **YOU** have a crush on anybody?

Ummmmm...

I kind of like *Hal*.

OOOOOOOOOH!

I learned **ALL** the best dirt on my sister that way.

Sometimes I imagined Sadie, Corina, and Bailey were MY best friends instead of Livy's.

POOF

But I knew I'd always be on the outside of their circle.

I was as outgoing as Olivia was shy, but I couldn't seem to find any friendships that stuck.

SCUFF SCUFF

Hey, guys, wanna play a game?

Hey, don't quit!
We were just joking!

24

The summer before we started fifth and sixth grade, my parents made an announcement.

Girls? Could you come in here for a moment? We have a **SURPRISE** for you!

Are we getting another dog? Can we name it Hercules?

You tell them.

No, you say it.

Before we started at Wilson Acres, my parents turned my mom's study into a bedroom for Olivia. It was small, but it was all hers.

32

I had a big bedroom all to myself, but I didn't want it. Without my sister to talk to, the dark seemed endless and scary.

I really missed her.

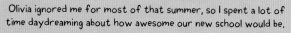

Olivia ignored me for most of that summer, so I spent a lot of time daydreaming about how awesome our new school would be.

CHAPTER 2

It wasn't only Olivia's hair and makeup that began to change. Some days, she wore clothes that seemed way too tiny...

Absolutely not, young lady. Go change.

But on other days, her clothes looked way too big.

Hey, Livy, did you mean to toss your whole sandwich?

THUMP

I noticed that she sometimes threw away perfectly good food.

I turned eleven a few months into the school year, and Mom took me to our pediatrician for my annual physical.

Hmm. Now, Lucy, what's your favorite food?

Tortellini. Just plain.

Plain? No sauce?

Nope. Plain.

Mmkay.

Do you play any sports?

Ummm, no. Not really.

What do you do during recess?

KICK KICK

I read.

Mmmhmmm.

Well, all right then! All good here.

Why don't you have a seat in the waiting room while your mother and I have a chat?

I lingered by the door because I wanted to hear what Dr. Douglas had to say about me. Except it wasn't **ME** they were talking about at all.

I'd like to check in about Olivia's recovery.

EXAM ROOM 3

That word "recovery" rattled me. If Olivia was **RECOVERING** from something, did that mean she was **SICK**?

No, no, no. It's not like that. It's not contagious, like the flu.

One big part of it all is that Olivia has a hard time dealing with change, and this switch to a new school has really been a challenge for her. She couldn't control that, though, so she became focused on her body, since it's one thing she CAN control. But then she started losing weight and she couldn't stop, and it snowballed from there.

Why didn't you tell me?

You're right. We should have told you, and I'm sorry you found out this way.

This is something for grown-ups to handle. We didn't want to worry you.

I'm not a baby.

I know.

Those two words sounded like a dark, scary spell. I felt like a bad sister for not knowing she was under this curse without me.

Stop staring at me, weirdo.

I studied Olivia for signs that she might be sick. She didn't cry or bleed. It didn't seem like she was in pain. There were no thermometers or casts.

Once I started paying attention, I realized sixth-grade Olivia dressed a lot differently than fifth-grade Olivia. Old Olivia was confident, but New Olivia just seemed like she wanted to disappear.

But noticing these changes didn't make me feel like I understood Olivia's eating disorder. In fact, it all just inspired even more questions.

I do! *See?* They're good. I'm eating them.

MMMMMMM

Mom, I like them!

Ugh. You're such a suck-up, Lucy.

I missed Livy, though. She made a few new friends in her class, and they spent most of their time walking around the mall and buying silly stuff like *lipgloss*.

Olivia + her new friends → conquering lip gloss mountain

SECRET SISTER CODE TRANSLATION:

Test, test, this is a test! Can you read this sentence?

I thought about teaching Eliza our secret sister code.

But if Eliza knew the code, then it wouldn't be a secret for sisters anymore.

ERASE
ERASE
ERASE

I wanted just one thing that only Livy and I could share.

I started hanging out at Eliza's house as much as I could because at home, no one had time for me anymore.

Hey, Mom, wanna make cookies with me?

Not now, sweetie, I have to take your sister to a doctor's appointment.

Have you seen my keys?

Will you help me draw an alligator?

Hold on just a moment, Dr. Cho.

What was that, Luce?

I asked if you could help me draw an alligator.

This call is important. Why don't you see if your sister wants to play?

I'm sorry, doctor. What did you say the cost for inpatient treatment is, if it comes to that?

Uh-huh. And they don't take insurance?

69

I started to like having my own room, after all. When I needed to get away from the drama, I escaped into books.

Mermaid Kingdom had always been my favorite series, but now I loved it even more.

MARY McNALLY — Mermaid Kingdom

MARY McNALLY — Mermaid Kingdom AND THE Coral Quest

MARY McNALLY — Mermaid Kingdom AND THE Aqua Deep

MARY McNALLY — Mermaid Kingdom AND THE Seahorse Castle

In the mermaid world, no one ever talked about dieting. And the mermaids only ate kelp, anyway, so what to eat was never an issue.

And mermaids always worked together to fix their problems, like the time Coral's pet clown fish, Bozo, swam away and all her friends banded together to help her find him.

I wished Livy would ask for **MY** help solving her problems, or that she'd offer to help me with mine. But I was like Coral at the beginning of the series.

One solitary mermaid, swimming alone.

I drew all the time, too. I started getting pretty good.

Except no one ever came to my room anymore, so the only person there to appreciate the art was me.

Olivia began to go to weekly appointments with nutritionists, psychiatrists, and eating disorder specialists. We spent a lot of time in doctors' offices.

I sat outside the room while Mom and Olivia met with doctors. Her appointments with Dr. Cho, the psychiatrist, were always the longest.

Time seemed to stop in those waiting rooms. Even reading and drawing didn't make the minutes go by faster.

I kept trying to wish Olivia better. I almost convinced myself it was working, until we took a trip to Florida for spring break. Suddenly, Olivia seemed to get **MUCH** sicker, very quickly. I couldn't deny it any longer.

We almost didn't go on the trip at all because of how much weight she'd lost, and she cried on the plane because it hurt to sit for longer than twenty minutes.

SECRET SISTER CODE TRANSLATION:

Are you okay?

Olivia and I shared a room on that trip. For the first time since I'd learned she was sick, I saw her body up close.

Without clothes, she looked like a skeleton.

Later...

RUMMAGE
RUMMAGE

ON THIN ICE

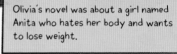

Olivia's novel was about a girl named Anita who hates her body and wants to lose weight.

She makes friends with a popular girl who eats a lot all at once and then throws it all back up. That was part of an eating disorder called *bulimia*.

Anita develops bulimia, too. By the end of the book, she's healthy again, and she learns a lesson about the dangers of dieting.

I knew the story meant to teach a lesson about unhealthy eating, but I read it as a way to finally understand my sister.

Our whole family seemed more exhausted after our trip than we did before we left.

Five minutes later...

Fifteen minutes later...

Thirty minutes later...

Finally...

I'LL eat her steak, okay?

UGH.

GET BACK HERE!

92

Later that night...

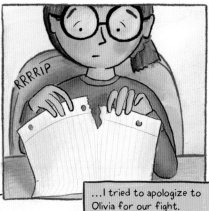

...I tried to apologize to Olivia for our fight.

RRRRIP

SECRET SISTER CODE TRANSLATION:

Dear Livy, I'm sorry I made you mad. I know it's none of my business. I just want you to feel better. Can we watch a movie together? I'll wait in my room. Love, Lucy

KEEP OUT

THWIP

Mom, Lexie's dad is here! He's dropping us off at the mall!

Okay, be home by dinner!

KEEP OUT

Olivia had stopped talking to me completely. It felt like a wall had formed between her and the rest of our family, and I was determined to break it down. In order to do that, I needed to know more about what was going on inside her head.

After reading *On Thin Ice*, I felt like I had a better idea of what to look for.

The body Olivia drew didn't look anything like her.

But it did kind of look like me.

CHAPTER 3

After our spring break trip, I started to think about my body differently. It seemed to come up more often in other people's conversations, too.

116

Old Olivia wore all the same stuff as me, but New Olivia's wardrobe was confusing. Before, I borrowed her stuff all the time. But now when I tried on her clothes, nothing fit right. I looked like a little kid playing dress-up.

Eliza was right. It was time I started changing up my look. I just needed to find my own way to do it.

Over the next few months, I noticed Olivia's habits start to change in small ways.

I'll just have **ONE**.

She began to eat foods she refused before, even though she still measured them first.

CRUN

Well, you know what they say when everyone at the table clears their plate. Tomorrow is gonna be a beautiful day!

She didn't leave anything on the plate after meals anymore, even though she didn't often look happy about it.

Sometimes, it seemed like she was getting sick all over again, but Mom said Olivia's brain and body each had to get better in their own ways and on their own time, and it wasn't easy.

That kind of progress could be frustrating, and we needed to be patient and help her through it.

Livy gained enough weight back to go to basketball camp, after all. Her hair began to grow back, too, thicker and curlier than before.

Hey, Luce!

Wanna look through the new issue of *Teen Beauty* with me later?

teenBEAUTY
FRESH SPRING
10 GREAT LOOKS
THE NEW FACES OF FASHION
HOW-TO OVERCOME ANXIETY

REALLY?!

Sometimes, she even started being nice to me again.

We know this has been a challenging couple of years for our family.

I don't like this at all.

And we know this might seem a bit sudden.

But we really hope you both think of this as an **ADVENTURE**!

My bosses offered me a huge promotion and a chance to open a new branch of the company.

We weren't expecting it at all, but it's an amazing opportunity!

It's too good to turn down.

We're moving, aren't we?

Maybe this was my chance to reinvent myself, just like Eliza and I talked about.

In a whole new state, I could *really* start fresh. Like Olivia when we switched schools the first time, this was my chance to discover **New Lucy!** I couldn't *wait* to meet her.

CHAPTER 4

JUNIORS

GIRLS

BOYS

ACTIVE

SALE SALE SALE SALE

Our new school had an intense dress code, so we had to get new clothes before school started. I'd done some thinking about what I wanted my new and improved image to be. I wanted to be colorful. I wanted to be fun. I wanted to be interesting.

A new, exciting wardrobe was the first step.

Try this on, Luce. I think it'll look nice on you.

I managed to find some clothes that were fun, affordable, and dress-code approved.

I especially loved my new, red plaid pants.

I couldn't wait for school to start.

I GOT IT!

BONK

My lies caught up with me quickly.

Kevin and Jack were the first two real friends I made at Thatcher. I'd never had friends who were *boys* before, but suddenly they seemed a lot less complicated than girls.

Kevin was outgoing and goofy. He wanted to be a famous comedian someday.

Who did the ghost take on a date?

Jack was quiet, smart, and really good at guitar.

Most of the guys at our school played hockey or surfed, and Jack and Kevin didn't do either of those things.

His *ghoul-friend!*

153

So, one week down! How did today go, Livy?

I **HATE** it here.

Luce? What about you?

It was...

...fine.

157

SECRET SISTER CODE TRANSLATION:
Livy, I'm sorry you're having a hard time getting used to Thatcher, but I am, too, and I just need someone to talk to. I miss the old you, the one who didn't think our games were stupid. Do you remember when we were best friends? I miss Eliza, and I miss Indy, and I miss our old house. You're the only person who could possibly understand.
Would you please talk to me?

RRRRRRIIIP

It was obvious Livy wasn't going to help me navigate this move.

CRUMPLE
CRUMPLE

TOSS

Guess I was gonna have to figure it all out by myself.

It was the first time I'd hung out with any of these girls outside of school, and I was sure it was my chance to make friends.

Happy birthday, Hannah!

Oh, hi, Lucy. You can just put that present over there.

Wow, that's really good.

Did you draw that?

You guys went as pop stars for Halloween, right? So I drew you as a pop star.

Someday when you're a famous artist we'll be able to say we knew you when!

All right, this next one is from . . . Blythe!

My plan was working!

When it came time for bed, Hannah announced there were assigned sleeping arrangements.

Blythe, Margo, Danielle, Sarah K, Amanda, Cady, and Min, you're sleeping in my room with me.

Everyone else, you're in the playroom.

Everyone in my room went to sleep right away, but the girls in Hannah's room stayed up talking.

Guys, can we just talk about something? Lucy is **SO** annoying.

172

175

SLAM

SLAM

STOMP
STOMP
STOMP

SLAM

I was devastated. I was *humiliated.* I finally understood why Livy wanted her own room so badly back in Indy. After Hannah's party, mine felt like the only place I'd ever be safe. And then, just when I was vowing to stay curled up on my bed until the end of time . . .

THWIP

for sister eyes only

FROM THE DESK OF
✳ OLIVIA HOWELL ✳

SECRET SISTER CODE TRANSLATION:
Hey, Luce, Are you okay? Mom said you tore up your favorite plaid pants. Why? Did something happen? I'm sorry I've been wrapped up in my own stuff since we started at Thatcher. Can I come in and talk to you?
Love, Livy.

178

CHAPTER 5

Over winter break, I decided to make some changes. I had a **Three-Phase Plan.**

Phase One required using my Christmas money to get some clothes that were more like the ones the popular girls wore. They weren't designer brands like theirs, but they weren't loud and obvious either.

SIGH

The new clothes were boring and didn't feel like me, but I decided to think of them as camouflage.

Phase Two was simple. I needed to make a friend—specifically, a friend who was a *girl*. I knew *just one girlfriend* would make everything easier.

That just left **Phase Three:** I was never going to be called chubby again.

HEY!

Do **NOT** feed the dog under the table.

Sorry.

But someone always seemed to be watching me.

BEEP BEEP BEEP

5:00

TIP TOE !!

MAPLE ALMOND GRANOLA MAPLE ALMOND GRANOLA HEALTH FLAKES CORN POOFS NUT LOUPS

PLOP

I tried to sneak around and make it look like I'd already eaten when I hadn't eaten anything . . .

Skylar had lots of ideas about ways to get thinner.

Maybe if we sleep with belts on, it will flatten our stomachs.

I'll just smell this instead of eating it.

Sky, this is just making me hungrier.

WAFT

WAFT

I don't know where she got these ideas, but none of them made any difference.

This says we need "heather from a wild river valley." Will dandelions from my yard work?

Double double, toil and trouble, make my butt look less like a bubble!

SPELLS FOR DUMMIES

LIVY'S NEW FRIEND, BRANDI.

Food's here!

Olivia was finally eating normally, most of the time.

Hey, Luce? All the rooms are full. Can I share yours?

Sure.

SIGH

Gaining weight. I know I wasn't healthy before. I **KNOW** that now.

But there's still that voice in my head sometimes that says I look horrible and it's all my fault.

I can at least recognize it's there now, but it doesn't totally go away, you know?

Are you guys done in there?

Yeah! Be right out!

Yeah. Actually, I do.

Skylar was always talking about what we **SHOULD** or **SHOULDN'T** eat, but her rules and ideas about what foods were "safe" seemed to change daily. Sometimes, it seemed easier to just eat nothing, but that had consequences, too.

For the first time in my life, I started to enjoy sports. But when I skipped meals, I was tired and lagged behind during practice. Sometimes, I even felt dizzy and faint.

Here! I'm open!

CRINKLE

SECRET SISTER CODE TRANSLATION:
Talk to me about how you're really feeling if you want. I won't tell Mom. I just don't want you to make the same mistakes I did.
Love, Livy

Later that night . . .

CHAPTER 6

I was putting so much thought and effort into changing my body, but it didn't occur to me that my body might just change on its own.

!!!

MOOOM!

Looks like a growth spurt to me.

That spring, I shot up five inches in four months. My bones grew so fast they actually ached.

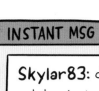

INSTANT MSG

Skylar83: do u think I should just ask kevin to the spring dance?
Skylar83: han thinks he likes me and he's just too scared to ask.

A A A A A **B** *I* U̲   link

Han?

INSTANT MSG

LucyXOXO719: idk, maybe.
Skylar83: has he said anything when i wasn't around about who he likes?

A A A A A **B** *I* U̲   link

Hoo, boy.

Luce? Why are you on the floor?

Can I ask you something?

Um, okay.

Are you better?

SIGH

Oh. Really?

I never just magically recovered. But I do know that Mom and Dad saved my life.

If they hadn't stuck with me, I don't think I ever would have gotten better.

How did it start? For you, I mean. Like, where did your eating disorder come from?

There isn't one huge moment that I can point to as the reason. I just always felt . . . big.

I've always been tall and I didn't want to be. And I thought I could reinvent myself at Wilson Acres.

Even when I lost some weight, I didn't feel small enough, though. So I just kept going.

Yeah. I thought I could reinvent myself at Thatcher, too.

Is that why you want to lose weight?

Yeah.

244

I think we're similar in a lot of ways, Luce.

Actually, I've always wished I could be more like you.

REALLY?!

When we were kids, I was super jealous that you weren't afraid to be different. You're talented, and you're funny, and you wear bold clothes just because you like them.

Don't let people like Hannah and Skylar make you feel ashamed to be you, okay? They're probably jealous, too.

Thanks, Livy.

Blech. You always ruin things with *hugs*.

When summer break started, I slept late every day.

Hey, sleepyhead. Get up. You're wasting the day.

CHAPTER 7

Now, I know this is a theater camp and you don't really do theater. But I think it'll be good for you to be around other creative people.

Just have an open mind, okay?

Camp Sunny was a two-week sleep-away camp. I was **NOT** excited to go.

CAMP SUNNY

I think you're going to have a **GREAT** time.

My summer was just starting to get interesting, and now I was going to be gone for two whole weeks. What if Jack forgot about me?

Trying to make friends at Thatcher had been so awful. The last thing I wanted to deal with was a whole new group of strangers.

All through dinner that first night, I just watched and listened. I wanted to suss out who the Hannahs and the Skylars were before getting in too deep.

Lily was quiet and sweet like Skylar when I'd first met her, but she wasn't shy at all.

So why'd you decide to come to Camp Sunny this summer?

Actually, my mom signed me up and kinda surprised me with it. I've never even done theater before!

Wait, you thought this was theater camp? It's a *circus* camp.

WHAT?

She's kidding. You get used to it.

Naomi was a little shy, but also had a sly, unexpected sense of humor.

Hope you're ready for some tightrope walking tomorrow.

The other two, Taylor and Iris, were outgoing and funny like Hannah, but they didn't seem the slightest bit mean.

And Pamela wasn't like anyone I'd ever met. I could tell right away that she was 100 percent herself.

For the first few days, I couldn't get Hannah and Skylar out of my head.

We'll start a new game if you wanna jump in!

Gross, no. That game is so dumb.

That bathing suit looks weird on your hips, Luce.

Grab a hairbrush! We're doing karaoke!

Lucy, you're SUCH a weird dancer.

Ew, who still listens to Ashley Sparks?

SECRET SISTER CODE TRANSLATION:
Dear Luce, I'm glad you're having fun at camp. You're right,
I would not like the hugs or the humidity. Want to plan a
shopping day with me before school starts when you get back
from camp? Your counselor sounds cool, but don't get any
ideas about replacing me. This town's only big enough for one
big sister, ya hear? Miss you. Love, Livy

P.S. Mom and I got you some candy to share
with your nerdy new friends. Enjoy.

P.P.S. No sisters are nice ALL the time, you know that!

P.P.P.S. Can you please just write Mom a letter and let her
know you're having fun so she quits bugging me about it?

Dear Lucy,

Haven't heard from you, so I hope that means you're having a blast!!!! Sending candy for you to share with your new camp friends, and a few new magazines for you to enjoy as well.

We all miss you so much. Please write back soon!

Love,
Mom ♡

Dear Mom,
Camp is awesome! Thanks for the candy and magazines. Really busy today but will write more soon. Love you!

✿△ℰ! ꙮ□⬚⋈,
ᕼ ✿⟍⚘⬯○○□◇! ꙮℰ⋈✿⚹⬤⚹✿
/!△ℰᕼ. ℰ◇✿ ✿⬤⋈◇'◇ ☆⚹♀!!⋈,
⬧!⬧△!△'⚹ ⬯⬤ !△◇♌ℰ ◯□◇/ ◇ ⟍△
⬚△ℰꙮ ◇⟍□◇!. ꙮ⚹⊠△,
ᕼℰ⚘⋈ ☺

**SECRET SISTER CODE
TRANSLATION:**
Dear Livy, A shopping day
sounds great. And don't
worry, there's no replacing
the real thing. Love, Lucy

↑

Howell
nny, Bowdoin
ake Rd
d, ME 03973

Taylor and Pamela were both in the top level dance class . . .

First . . .

Second . . .

Third . . .

Fourth . . .

Uhhhh . . .

I was still having a hard time remembering fifth position.

Dear Lucy,

What's up? Hope camp is fun. I'm bummed we didn't get to hang out more this summer but I'm excited for school to start. Do you know what section you'll be in next year? Probably not because you're at camp, haha. I'm in 702.

I also wanted to ask you something. I know Kevin asked you to go to a movie and you said no because of Skylar, but I was wondering if maybe it was also because you like someone else? Because I like you, lol. Would you maybe want to be my girlfriend when you get back from camp? Pretty lame of me to write it in a letter, haha. But I was kinda nervous to ask you in person and my brother told me letters are romantic. Write back if you want!

Sincerely, Jack

Our cabin had been practicing a dance to a funky '80s song all week. On the night of the show, we all got ready together.

What did you do?

What **COULD** I do? The other girl got the solo, and I went home and hated myself.

The thing that teacher said that stung the most was that even if I lost weight, I still wouldn't ever be right. My body ruled me out, no way around it.

Dieting seemed useless if there wasn't even hope there. So I quit dance and started finding other ways to punish my body for what it wouldn't let me have.

Like what?

Doesn't matter. Not the point.

The point IS, before things got really bad, my grandma noticed. She's a dancer, too—not ballet, but she's been a teacher for years. She confronted me and I broke down and told her everything. And you know what she said? She said—

Every person has a body, Luce. No matter what size you are, you can only get so much bigger or so much smaller. If you're constantly worried about making yourself thinner, then you're defined by something that is literally the opposite of growth.

And girl, you gotta **GROW**!

But that's just it! I feel like, at camp, I'm starting to . . .

Like, I've been worried for a long time about how I look. But I'm realizing that I can't **DO** anything special either.

Everybody has a thing but me. You know dancing is your thing, no matter what some dance teacher says.

Are you maybe a little hung up on this **THING** thing?

Our cabin's act was up first. My dancing **WAS** totally off beat, but I had so much fun, it didn't matter.

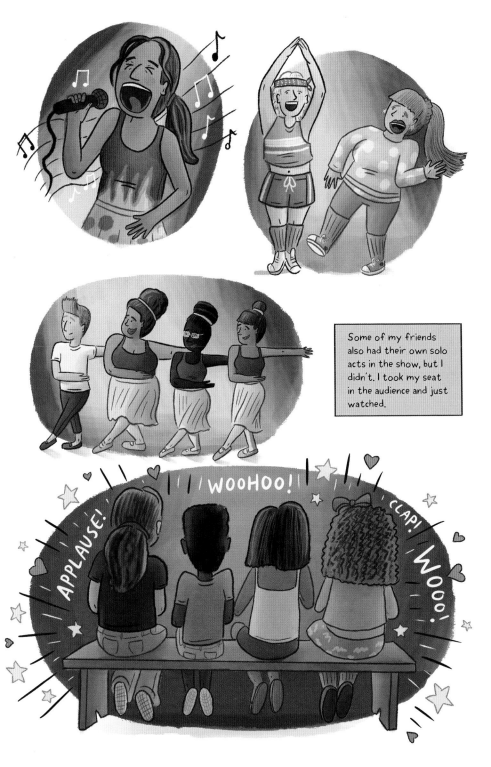

Some of my friends also had their own solo acts in the show, but I didn't. I took my seat in the audience and just watched.

There were so many different ways to be talented, and I started to wonder if it only seemed like everyone else had found their **THING** because I was looking at them from the outside. All these talented people probably had their own problems and insecurities I couldn't see.

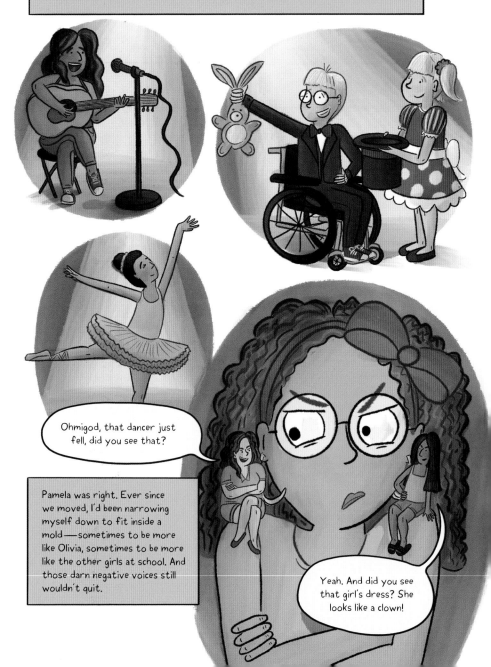

Ohmigod, that dancer just fell, did you see that?

Pamela was right. Ever since we moved, I'd been narrowing myself down to fit inside a mold—sometimes to be more like Olivia, sometimes to be more like the other girls at school. And those darn negative voices still wouldn't quit.

Yeah. And did you see that girl's dress? She looks like a clown!

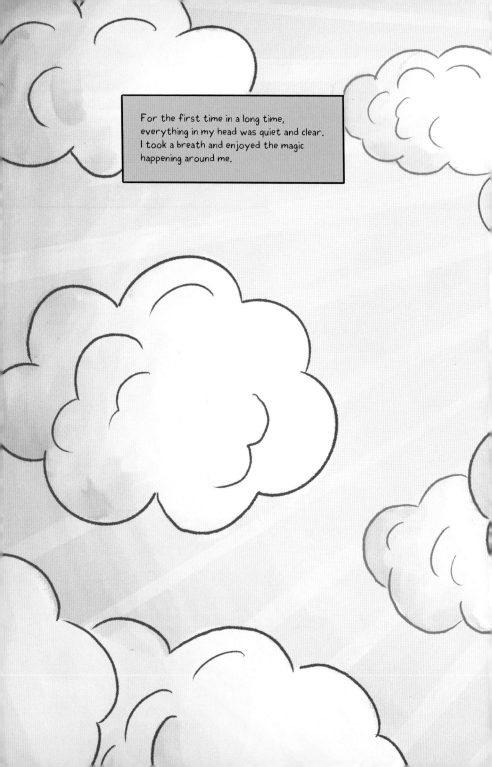

For the first time in a long time,
everything in my head was quiet and clear.
I took a breath and enjoyed the magic
happening around me.

Camp Sunny didn't exactly change me, but it did change my perspective. Suddenly, a world that had seemed so small and dark and hopeless felt bright and full of opportunity.

It was up to me to forge the path from here.

After camp, my Thatcher friend problems didn't seem quite so scary.

None of my friends from camp went to my school, but just the fact they existed was a reminder that there were people out there in the world that were a fit for me, even if Hannah and Skylar weren't.

My post-camp glow didn't overhaul how I saw my body. I didn't come back a new person after two weeks in the woods. Like Olivia said, that kind of change takes time. It was more that I wasn't afraid to go into a new school year feeling *different*. For the first time in a while, that felt like a good thing.

AUTHOR'S NOTE

Dear Reader,

Smaller Sister is not a memoir, but it is inspired by real events. My older sister, Katie, was diagnosed with an eating disorder when I was ten and she was twelve. At the time, I struggled to understand why my best friend changed seemingly overnight into someone I didn't know, and I found the complexities of this cruel disease that upended my family as I knew it hard to understand. I loved her and I was scared for her, but I was also mad at her. I was jealous of the attention she received and envious of the way she looked even when I knew it was unhealthy. I looked up to her, and yet I didn't want to be anything like her. But most of all, I wanted my REAL sister to come back, and I wanted my family to go back to the cohesive unit it was before.

But it was by moving forward, not backward, that I eventually got my sister back. Today, Katie is a great writer who runs half marathons, is an expert at doing makeup, and very irritatingly picks all the good parts out of every box of cereal. She is much, much more than a disease.

Like Lucy, I also developed disordered eating in the wake of my sister's eating disorder, and real change didn't happen in the way I saw myself until I started accepting myself as valuable for more than just what I looked like. These days, as a grown-up, my habits are a lot healthier, but those critical voices are still there. I try not to give them too much say, but it isn't easy, and every day is a new conversation.

The thing about bodies is that you only get one. Much like a pesky sister, you have to live with it every single day even when you'd rather trade it in for one you might like better. But it's also just one part of you and, as Pamela says, "no matter what size you are, you can only get so much bigger or so much smaller." And you gotta GROW.

If you or someone you love is struggling with disordered eating, anxiety, or depression, you're not alone. There are great resources available to you, including:

Active Minds: activeminds.org

National Alliance on Mental Illness (NAMI): nami.org

National Eating Disorder Association: nationaleatingdisorders.org

Multi-Service Eating Disorder Association: medainc.org

♡ Maggie

SHH!

SECRET SISTER CODE
TRANSLATOR
Write your own secret notes with this handy key!

SOME FUN EXTRA STUFF!

These are the annual First Day of School photos with my sister, Katie, that my mom took on our front steps in St. Louis, MO, that inspired the cover!

Kindergarten (me) and 1st grade (Katie)

5th grade (me) and 6th grade (Katie)

2nd grade (me) and 3rd grade (Katie)

A real diary entry of mine from 5th grade that shows how true to life the sister feelings in this book are!

Dear Diary,
Oh my gosh! My sister must take lessons on being annoying.

ACKNOWLEDGMENTS

THANK YOU SO MUCH!

First of all, thank you to my sister, Katie, and to my mom, Laurie, for letting me spin a fictional version of our story.

To the rest of my Edkins family—Dad, Jess, Grandma Margie, Ryan, Tim, Viola, Fritz, Penny, and Ruby. To Sue, Tim, and my lil bro, Brian—I am so lucky to be a Willis. To the extended Campbell, Callahan, Willis, and Campilii clans for all your love and support.

To my superhero agent, Jennifer Rofé of Andrea Brown Literary Agency, and to her assistants, Kayla and Adah, for not flinching when I dropped a graphic novel script on you out of nowhere. You somehow always say exactly the right thing to shepherd me where I need to go, and I'm so happy to be on this wild ride of publishing with you. To my brilliant editors, Megan Abbate and Connie Hsu, for championing this story and for helping me shape it into something far better. To the rest of Team *Smaller Sister* at Roaring Brook/Macmillan: Nicolás Oré-Girón, Kirk Benshoff, Molly Johanson, Jen Besser, Allison Verost, Mary Van Akin, Kristen Luby, Elysse Villalobos, Jen Healey, Taylor Pitts, Allene Cassagnol, Molly Ellis, and Mariel Dawson for your tireless work to make this book the best it can be and to get it in the hands of readers.

To my critique group—Kristin Standley, Samira Iravani, Krista Ahlberg, Helen Seachrist, and Ashley Christiano—for sharing your words and wise feedback. To Jen Keenan, my publishing buddy. To all my colleagues and mentors at Penguin Young Readers and Little, Brown for teaching me so much about books and art over the last decade. To Amanda and Barbara Bakowski, Joy Allen, Liz Ballantyne, Justin Moore, Ashley Weyl, Courtney Strickland, Maya Callender, and Kate Carroll for always being there with a hug and a dog pic. To the Princeton Tiger community, and to all my Penn friends and teachers.

Thank you to my readers, and especially to all the Lucys out there. Your plaid pants ARE cool.

And most of all, thank you to my best friend and soulmate, Mike, for reading all those drafts, for narrating the action on TV when I was too busy drawing to pay attention, and for picking up Tico's on your way home. You and Mutzy are my heart. Thank you for lovin' me.

Me and my two REAL-LIFE older sisters, Katie (left) and Jess (middle).

© 2022 Kimberly Powers

MAGGIE EDKINS WILLIS was born in St. Louis, Missouri, and grew up in southern Maine. She designed and art directed books for children's publishers for seven years before embarking on a career crafting stories of her own. She now lives in Princeton, New Jersey, with her husband, a college football coach, and their husky mix, Mozzarella. When she's not writing or drawing, you can usually find her reading, running, or botching muffin recipes.

maggiemadethis.com